Disney
MEET THE ROBINSONS

Keep Moving Forward

Adapted by Katherine Emmons
Illustrated by Ron Husband and The Disney Storybook Artists
Designed by Disney Publishing's Global Design Group

HarperEntertainment
An Imprint of HarperCollinsPublishers

Meet the Robinsons: Keep Moving Forward

Copyright © 2007 Disney Enterprises, Inc.

RADIO FLYER is a registered trademark of Radio Flyer, Inc. and is used with permission.

Library of Congress catalog card number: 2006937693

ISBN-10: 0-06-112469-9 — ISBN-13: 978-0-06-112469-3

❖

First Edition

Hi! I'm Wilbur Robinson, son of the famous Cornelius Robinson, Founder of the Future and Time Machine inventor. Of course, that's in the future, and you're not there yet. So let's start at the beginning.

Way back in the past—before I was born—my dad was found on the front steps of an orphanage. He was just a baby. Everyone called him Lewis.

Lewis wanted a family. But he had a hard time finding one.

Maybe it was because even though Lewis was a total genius, he didn't connect with other people very well.

Mildred, the nice lady who ran the orphanage, always had high hopes for Lewis. She knew that someday he would find a family of his own.

Some of his early inventions were great! He created the first Peanut-Butter-and-Jelly Sandwich Maker. Could anybody have guessed that in the future, the hat would be used everywhere?

And then there was his Perpetual Popcorn Machine with its super-blaster attachment. The attachment had one little problem, but nobody seemed to mind.

Lewis had given up on being adopted. He thought his only chance for a family was to find his real mother. So Lewis invented a Memory Scanner to remember her, find her, and convince her to keep him.

And, boy, did he work hard to build that Memory Scanner. At last, it was ready, so Lewis headed off to the school science fair to show his new invention.

The Memory Scanner didn't work out quite the way he planned. It broke and pieces of it flew across the room. This was not Lewis's fault, by the way. It was part of a plan hatched by the Bowler Hat Guy and his diabolical hat, Doris, to steal the Memory Scanner and change the future. Now that would have been a *real* disaster.

Anyway, Lewis didn't know all this. He just felt like
a failure and he was ready to give up.

That's when I entered the picture. I came from the future in my dad's Time Machine. (Pretty cool, huh?) I found Lewis and took him to the future. He was a little freaked out at first.

But I stuck to my plan and encouraged Lewis to find his confidence.

Then I hit a snag. See, my goofy family liked him so much that they decided to adopt him!

The problem was that if he stayed in the future, he would never grow up to be my dad! I had to tell everybody the truth.

Once Lewis realized that my family was his destiny, he knew that to move forward, he had to go back.

He went right back to the science fair, where he fixed the Memory Scanner and met some terrific people: my grandparents! Weird, huh?

As Lewis grew up to be Cornelius Robinson he kept making great inventions: Bubble Transport Systems, Magnetic Monorails, and Flying Cars. The future became a terrific place.

Keep Moving Forward.
That's my dad's motto. After all, it's
what turned his life around. Once he got
a glimpse of the future, he kept looking
forward and never looked back.

My dad never did get that popcorn machine
to work right, but that's okay.

The whole family kind of likes it the way it is—especially Grandpa.

And speaking of my family, they're in the future and I'd better get back there. Actually, it's the present for me, but the future for you. Got it? You'll understand some day. See you in a few decades!